ALSO BY TIM WYNNE-JONES

The Boy in the Burning House
Stephen Fair
Lord of the Fries
The Book of Changes
Some of the Kinder Planets
The Maestro
The Last Piece of Sky
Zoom Upstream
The Hour of the Frog
Mischief City
Architect of the Moon
I'll Make You Small
Zoom Away
Zoom at Sea

NED MOUSE BREAKS AWAY

THE
GOVERNMEN
IS UNFAIR
TO MICE

NED MOUSE BREAKS AWAY

TIM WYNNE-JONES

PICTURES BY

DUŠAN PETRIČIĆ

A GROUNDWOOD BOOK

Groundwood Books / Douglas & McIntyre
720 Bathurst Street, Suite 500, Toronto, Ontario M5S 2R4

We acknowledge the support of the Canada Council for the Arts, the Ontario Arts Council and the Government of Canada through the Book Publishing Industry Development Program for our publishing activities.

National Library of Canada Cataloguing in Publication Data
Wynne-Jones, Tim
Ned Mouse breaks away
ISBN 0-88899-474-5
I. Petričić, Dušan II. Title
PS8595.Y59N42 2002 jC813'.54 C2001-904166-7
PZ7.W993Ne 2002

Design by Michael Solomon
Printed and bound in Canada

To Herman Bianchi

and his lifetime of research into

a non-punitive system of crime control.

1

Ned Mouse did not like jail. He did not like his tiny cell. He did not like the food. And he did not look good in stripes.

"I would give my right arm to be out of here," he thought.

And so, the very next day he took a dessert spoon from the cafeteria. That night when the other prisoners were asleep, he started to dig a tunnel from his cell.

He tunneled down, down, down.

He tunneled across, across, across.

And when he was quite sure he was outside the walls of the prison, he tunneled...well, you can guess.

Unfortunately, he tunneled right into the warden's house.

Even then, Mouse might have escaped. The warden was so busy eating his dinner that he didn't even notice his uninvited guest. But on the sideboard stood a bowl of chocolate tiramisu.

Did they serve the prisoners chocolate tiramisu? Are you kidding?

How Mouse's mouth watered. "Just one taste," he told himself. But one taste led to another and another and then...

"Guard!" yelled the warden. "There's a mouse in my tiramisu!"

Before Mouse had time for another bite, he was nabbed.

"How foolish I have been," he grumbled to himself. "I should never have equipped myself for this expedition with a dessert spoon."

The guard was as big as a tree. He hoisted Mouse under his stout arm and carried him back to his cell.

"You prisoners are all alike," he said. "All you think about is getting out of here."

"Wouldn't you?" said Mouse.

The guard looked surprised. "Why would I want to get out of here?" he said. "I have a good job."

Mouse shook his head. "The brains of a tree," he thought.

"I am your keeper," said the guard, when he had locked Mouse back in his cramped little cell. “Because that’s my job, to keep you in.”

“We’ll see about that,” said Mouse.

2

What was Ned Mouse's crime, you ask?

Not finishing his spinach.

"But that's not a crime," you say. "Sometimes I don't finish my spinach and I'm no criminal."

Ah, but do you write in your unfinished spinach with your finger? Do you write nasty things about the government? Things like, "The government is unfair to mice!" You see, that is what Mouse did. And he didn't do it just once, either. He did it again and again. And sometimes, just for a change, he wrote in his pureed squash or in his custard, "The government is unfair to mice!" And the government didn't like it one bit.

And so off to jail he went. "And throw away the key!" said the judge.

"Hah!" thought Ned Mouse. "Who needs a key?"

He was always thinking of escape. Why, the very day after the bad dessert incident, Mouse started building an airplane in shop class. Out of tin.

"What is that?" asked the keeper.

"A washing machine," said Mouse.

The keeper looked it over with a

puzzled expression on his face. "It has pretty big wings for a washing machine," he said.

"What a mind," thought Mouse. "Pure mahogany."

As soon as the airplane was finished, Mouse took it down to the yard at recess.

"Why are you taking that washing machine out to the yard?" asked the keeper.

"Why indeed," said Mouse, thinking quickly. "Uh, in case one of the prisoners falls in the mud and gets his pants dirty?"

The keeper smiled. "That is very thoughtful of you," he said.

Mouse rolled his eyes. Could there

be such a gullible soul in the whole world?

As soon as he was in the yard, he wheeled his airplane to the farthest corner. He yelled, “Heads up!” to the other inmates, then jumped into the cockpit and turned on the motor.

Rmmmm, rmmmm, rmmmm.

Mouse let out the brake. The airplane rattled and bumped across the yard. Then it was in the air, climbing, climbing. He could hear the inmates cheering below. Higher and higher he rose, until...

Clunk!

His wheels caught on the top of the wall and down he plummeted.

Crash! Crunch!

The keeper carried him back to his cell. “Maybe you didn’t have enough spin on the rinse cycle,” he said.

“The rinse cycle,” grumbled Mouse. “Perfect.”

3

Many months passed, but did Mouse give up? Not on your life.

"Jail is not for the likes of me," he said to anyone who would listen. "Jail is for dangerous criminals. Maniac mink who chatter on cell phones while driving their cars. Willful weasels who pilfer your skipping rope. Cavalier coyotes who splash through puddles when you're in your Sunday suit." But no one would listen.

"I'll get out of here if it kills me," vowed Mouse.

He tried escaping down the garbage chute. He tried escaping down the laundry chute. He tried escaping down the drain hole in the tub. But somehow the keeper always found him and carried him back to his cell.

Once he made an extra-large vacuum cleaner in shop. Out of tin. He was very good with tin.

When the keeper wasn't looking, Mouse climbed inside the vacuum cleaner. He had left a note pinned to the hose.

Keeper,
I'd like you to carry this super new industrial-strength vacuum cleaner to my house and just leave it by the front steps so the gardener might clean my driveway when he has the time.
The warden.

The keeper always did as he was told, and so he took the vacuum cleaner directly to the warden's house which was, as you will remember, outside the walls of the jail.

Mouse heard the mighty door of the jail open and close.

"Perfect!" he thought inside his cramped chamber. "It won't be long now."

Splonk!

The keeper put down the vacuum.

"Now, back to your rounds," thought Mouse excitedly.

But just then, with a huge roar, the machine sprang to life.

"You were just supposed to leave it!" yelled Mouse.

But it was too late. Suddenly the industrial-sized vacuum cleaner was sucking up dust and dirt and stones and leaves and old rakes and basketballs and rose bushes.

"Ouch! Ouch! Ouch!" yelled Mouse. "Get me out of here!"

The vacuum cleaner stopped. The keeper opened the door and peered inside. He plucked out Mouse and held him up by his striped britches. Mouse wriggled and punched the air.

"Let me down, you ironwood, you rock elm, you coconut! You were just supposed to leave it for the gardener. Can't you read?"

"It was such a lovely day," said the keeper. "And it gets so gloomy in the jail."

"Tell me about it," squawked Mouse.

The keeper beamed. "It's lucky I was here, isn't it?"

"Lucky for whom?" said Mouse.

"For you," said the keeper. "Or who would have rescued you from the vacuum cleaner?"

"How does he do it," grumbled Ned Mouse to himself.

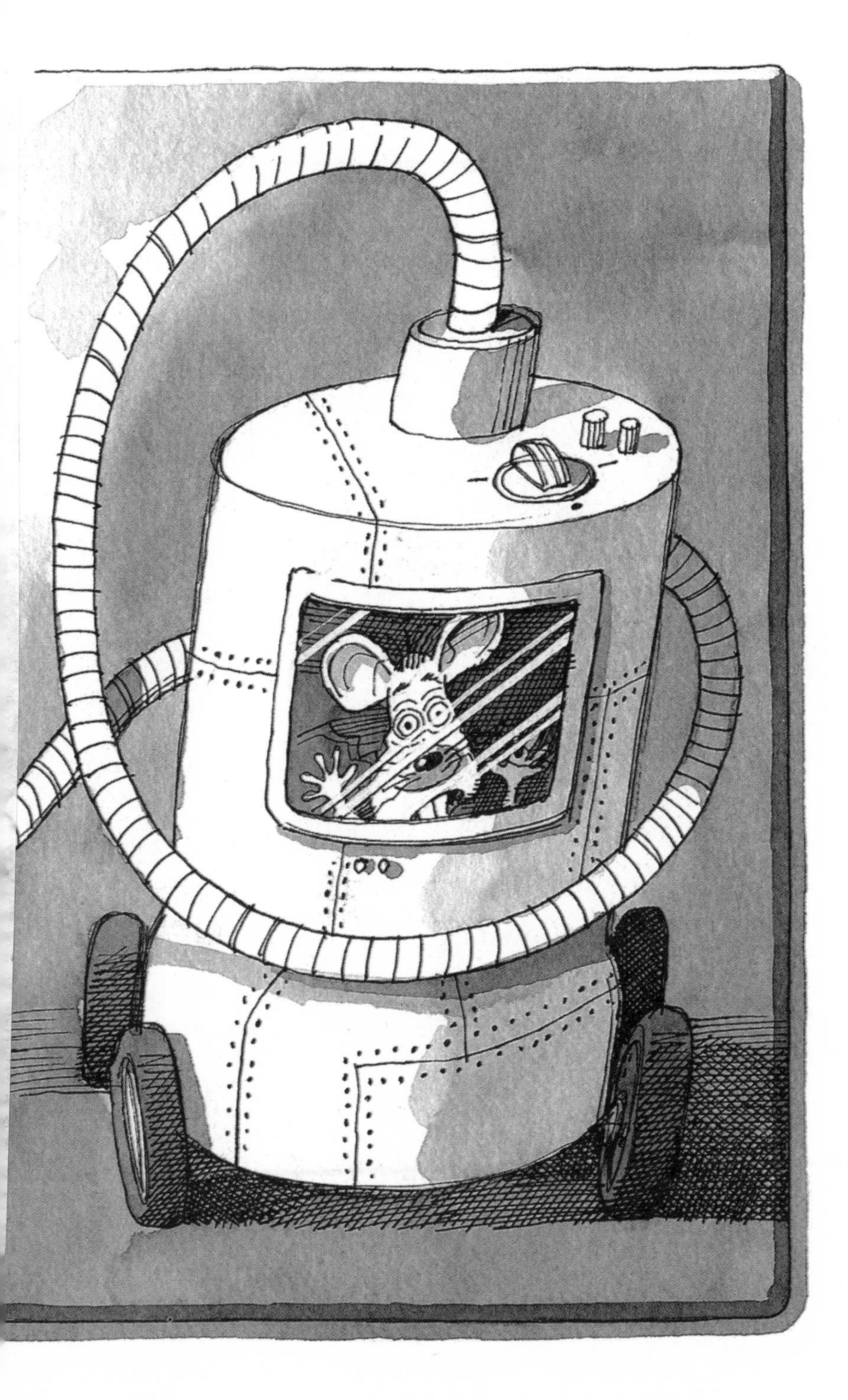

4

As time passed, Mouse became more and more desperate. He couldn't remember what it was like to feel the rain on his face. He couldn't remember what a roasted marshmallow tasted like.

"I can't take much more of this," he said.

Books helped. There was a library in the jail. Not a big one, but one day he found a childhood favorite, *The Wind in the Willows*.

"Ah, Ratty," he thought. "Now there was a great rodent."

But it was Toad who inspired Mouse on this particular reading. Toad (the rascal) in jail himself but escaping by dressing up as a washerwoman.

"A washerwoman," thought Mouse. "Perfect!"

That very afternoon, he made a dress in sewing class. The next day, he made a wig in hairdressing class. Finally, on the weekend, he made a nice big wicker basket in basket-weaving class.

"Keep," he called in his best impersonation of a washerwoman's voice. "I'm ready to take away this big stinky pile of clothes."

And he almost made it, except that the keeper, who followed him out, accidentally stepped on his skirt.

Riiiiiip!

Off it came.

"Wait a minute," said the keeper. "Washerwomen don't wear striped pajamas."

He nabbed Mouse, but he didn't carry him back to his cell right away. He seemed to be thinking.

It took him a long time to think.

"Wait a minute," he said again at

long last. "We don't even have washer-women."

Mouse mumbled, "Keep, my friend, do you realize that you have the mental capacity of a gum tree?"

The keeper smiled. "I like gum," he said.

5

Years passed. And slowly, Mouse lost the will to escape. But then, one dark and dreary day, he received a letter from his long-lost friend Morty. Morty had been looking for him everywhere, and he had finally tracked him down. He had written to ask after Mouse and to say that he had moved to a house by the sea.

"Oh, you should see it, Ned. What a view! What beautiful sunrises!"

Now, that might seem to you a heartless thing to say to a mouse in jail for life, if Mort hadn't added, "And I know you will see it, my dear friend. Somehow you'll get away. I'm writing letters to the government. I'm telling my friends. What you wrote in the spinach all those years ago was nothing less than the truth. Many of us felt that way, but few had the nerve to say it. You are a hero, Neddy, not a criminal. And when you are free, you must come straight to me. Why, you could help me at my new doll factory. In the meantime, here's a dollar to buy yourself some chocolate."

Mort had remembered how much Ned Mouse loved chocolate.

Eagerly, Ned looked inside the envelope. He gasped. There was no dollar.

Mouse rattled the door of his cell.

"Keep!" he yelled. "Somebody stole my chocolate money."

The keeper looked sorrowful. "It wasn't me," he said.

"Then who was it?" demanded Mouse.

The keeper looked ashamed. "The warden took it," he whispered through the bars. "To pay you back for eating his tiramisu."

"That was seventeen years ago," cried Mouse. Then he sat down on his little bed and wept. "It's not fair," he said. "They always open our letters."

"They have to," said the keeper.

"Why?" asked Mouse between sobs.

The keeper leaned his huge face against the bars of the cell. "Well, to make sure there isn't a file inside that you could use to file your way through the bars. Or maybe a shovel or a machine gun or maybe even a bull-dozer."

"That would be some letter," grumbled Mouse. He wasn't crying anymore. He was in one almighty huff. "Stealing isn't nice."

The keeper nodded. "I think you're right," he said.

"What?" said Mouse, hardly able to believe his ears.

"It isn't fair," said the guard.

"So why am I in here?" asked Mouse.

The keeper scratched his head. Then he smiled. He knew the answer. "Because you're a criminal," he said.

"Criminal schriminal!" said Mouse, jumping on the little table beside the cell door. "I'm not dangerous. I don't splash people or steal things. And I don't even own a cell phone."

"No," said the keeper. You don't."

"You see," said Mouse. "We need somewhere to keep the really nasty ones. And maybe jail is the best we can do. How many dangerous criminals are in this jail?"

The keeper scratched his head again and started counting on his fingers. "Probably a dozen," he said.

"Ah hah!" said Mouse. "And how many *un*dangerous criminals are there in this jail. How many, pray tell?"

Again the guard smiled. "I know the answer," he said, clapping his hands with glee. "Seven thousand, four hundred and eighty-nine."

Then, before Mouse could say, "Ah hah!" or "You see what I mean!" or "Now, we're getting somewhere!" the keeper simply walked away.

"Wait!" yelled Mouse. "I'm trying to tell you something. This jail is a huge waste of time and money when there are only a few really bad people in it."

But the keeper was gone. Mouse watched him leave, stupefied.

"Why do I even try?" he said to himself.

He slumped, alone and desolate on his cot. The book he was reading, *Our Mouse in Havana*, no longer held his interest.

"They open your letters and steal your chocolate money," he said. Then suddenly he sat straight up.

"But they don't open the letters you send out."

An idea began to brew in his brainy little head. "Yes!" he thought. "I'll make it this time."

The next morning, Mouse called for his keeper in a very cheery voice.

"Keep," he said, "I'll need some stamps and some wrapping paper — lots of wrapping paper — and some string."

"All right," said the keeper, smiling. He was glad to see Mouse in a better mood.

Mouse started small: some claws, a

whisker or two, and his funny bone. He had never liked his funny bone, anyway. He wrapped these few things up nice and sturdy with a good knot and mailed the package off to his friend Mort, with a letter explaining his plan.

The next week he received a letter from Mort. It was written in code, so as not to give away the plan.

"Thanks so much for the lovely puzzle you are making for me in shop. I can't wait for the next installment."

"That's nice, making your friend a puzzle," said the keeper, who had read Mort's letter.

The next day, Mouse handed the keeper a slightly larger package. Inside were his left eye and his left ear. He had made replacements in shop class.

What did he need two ears and two eyes for in a jail? The scenery wasn't any good, and he had heard all the jokes the prisoners told a million times.

One eye and one ear were enough, for the time being. Meanwhile, how happy his other eye and ear would be at Mort's house, looking out to sea and listening to the sea-gulls cry.

"What's this?" asked the keeper, shaking the package on the third day. It was bigger still.

"A machine gun," said Mouse.

"Ha-ha-ha," said the keeper, and he walked away with the package. Mouse watched it go with a sinking feeling. For inside the package was his little heart.

On the fourth day, the keeper said,

"Is this more of the puzzle? It sure seems heavy."

"Actually, it's a bulldozer," said Mouse.

The keeper laughed. "You're a funny one," he said.

"Just light-hearted," said Mouse.

And so, bit by bit, Mouse mailed himself away.

He mailed away his insides.

"You don't look so good," said the keeper.

"I'm on a diet," said Mouse.

Then he mailed away his legs. He had made a replacement pair in shop.

"You're limping," said the keeper with genuine concern. "Are you sure you're all right?"

"Ah, it's nothing a little holiday by the sea wouldn't cure," said Mouse.

"You have a good sense of humor," the keeper said.

Mouse winked at him with his one real eye. "I'll be sure to leave it behind for you when I'm done with it," he said.

7

What an extraordinary escape, you are thinking. How could he do it, tear himself apart like that? Well, you have never spent any time in prison, or you would understand. Every day Mouse sent Mort a little bit more of himself. It felt good. He felt lighter and lighter.

But he was becoming more and more impatient.

“It isn’t healthy being in two places

at once like this," he mumbled to himself, thinking of all the parts of him that were now at Mort's place.

How he longed to be by the sea. He could smell it. That was because he had already mailed off his nose. He wore a fake nose in its place. It was, as you have probably guessed, made of tin, and it wasn't all that comfortable.

With grim determination he decided. "It's time to get this escape over with."

And so he worked like a demon in shop the next day. This was the hard part. How was he to mail the last bits off? He needed one good eye to see what he was doing. And, of course he needed his brain and his arms to wrap things and write the correct address on the package. How terrible it would be if some part of him was sent somewhere else!

No, it didn't bear thinking about. But that was the trouble with having a brain.

"Ah," thought Mouse, "the brain does think terrible, awful things from time to time, but it also thinks up poems and jokes. And, best of all, clever escape plans."

Finally, it came down to the next-to-last shipment.

"Keep, Keep, I've got another package for you."

The voice sounded like Mouse. But it was only a recording. For in the package on the little table by the cell door was the rest of Mouse's body, including his voice.

When the keeper arrived, he saw the prisoner lying in his cot with his blanket pulled right up to his chin. It was a tin chin. Mouse had made an exact replica of himself, and it was lying in bed with a tape machine in its head. It was all tin from top to toe, except for his right arm.

"Your voice sounds funny," said the keeper.

"A little tinny, do you think?" said Mouse. "A head cold. I hardly feel myself."

Mouse had figured out exactly what the keeper would say and had recorded all the right answers with long enough pauses for the slow-witted

guard to think of what he was going to say next.

Then the keeper suddenly said, “Wow!”

He had only just seen the package. It was sitting right under his nose, but he had been so concerned to see Mouse in bed that he hadn’t noticed it.

“This is the biggest one of all,” said the keeper. He sounded suspicious. “Are you sure this is just a puzzle?”

“It’s Mort’s birthday,” said Mouse’s recorded voice, “and I’m sending him a cake.”

“Wow!” said the keeper again. He opened the door of the cell and picked

up the package. He was just going to shake it, when Mouse's recorded voice interrupted him.

"Don't shake it, Keep, if you please. I've already lit the candles and they might go out."

"Oh," said the keeper, holding the package very still.

But he didn't go right away. He walked through the dim light of the cell to the side of Mouse's bed. He sat down on the edge of it, very carefully. What little light there was glistened on the mouse's tin face.

"You look chilled," said the keeper. "Here, let me put another blanket on you."

And with that, he put the package on the floor, as carefully as he could. Which wasn't quite carefully enough.

"Owww!" said a muffled voice.

"Sorry," said the keeper. He looked around. Where had *that* voice come from? It seemed to have come from the package. He picked it up again. He held it close to his ear. He began to untie the string.

"Rats!" thought Mouse inside the package. "Now I'm done for." But he didn't dare speak, or the keeper would know where he was.

Then suddenly the keeper stopped untying the package.

"That was close!" he said, turning to the tin mouse lying in the bed. He grinned. "You trickster. If I had opened it, I might have burned myself on all those candles."

Inside the package, Mouse breathed a little sigh of relief. It was hard to believe anyone could be so dull-witted, and yet, the keeper was really very kind.

"I'm going to miss him," he thought. And what a surprise that was. "Goodbye, old Keep," he whispered very, very quietly. "Thanks for all your help."

But the keeper still didn't leave. Again he put down the package — very carefully this time — and tucked in the little prisoner in the bed.

How rigid he seemed. How lifeless.

And that made the keeper sad. And his sadness made him think.

Now, the keeper didn't do much thinking, as well you know. It wasn't his job to think. It was his job to make sure prisoners didn't get away.

But a terrible and wonderful thing

happened to him just then. He realized that he had come to love the little mouse. He had never met anyone like Ned. He had never met anyone with so much life in him. And now here he lay on a jail-cell cot looking like...well, like something made in shop class.

"I think maybe you were right, Mouse," he said. "It isn't fair."

8

The next morning when he went to check on his prisoner, the keeper found Mouse lying perfectly still in his bed. It was the tin mouse, of course. Almost entirely.

In Mouse's cell, on the little table by the door, there was a note.

Dear Keep,
I wonder if you could do me a big favor. Could you possibly wrap up my right arm—the one with the pen in it—and mail it to my dear friend, Mort. He's going through a bad bout of arthritis, so I thought I might lend him a hand (ha-ha). It's the least a friend can do.
Yours,
Ned

The keeper was touched by such generosity. A tear plopped on the note, making it hard to read the postscript.

P.S. I hope there is enough paper and string left over:

9

It was a perfect blue-sky day. The ocean sparkled and the vision of it sparkled in Mouse's eyes. (Yes, his two eyes were back together again. There was no distance between them anymore. Except, of course, his nose.) He was complete. Almost. The keeper had never sent him his right arm.

"Oh, well," he said stoically. "I did

say I would give my right arm to be free."

He was lounging on the deck drinking an icy-cold walnut cream soda pop while Mort grilled up some red onions, yellow peppers and purple eggplant on the barbecue. It was early closing day at Morty's Doll Factory, and the two friends were enjoying a leisurely lunch. They needed the break. Things were hopping at the factory.

"We're way behind in shipping," said Mort, expertly flipping a pepper. We're getting more orders than we can handle thanks to your fabulous new robot toys, Mouse."

Mouse smiled. "It's great to be working," he said.

Mort was about to say, "Isn't that the truth," when suddenly he put his hand to his eyebrow to shield out the sun and peered down the beach.

Someone was coming. Someone very large.

"Uh-oh," said Mort.

Mouse followed his gaze.

"It's him," he said. He could tell by the lumbering walk that it was the keeper. Except that he wasn't in uniform. He was wearing Italian sunglasses, a Hawaiian shirt, Bermuda shorts and Mexican sandals.

Mort growled and turned toward the approaching intruder, spatula at the ready.

"He tries anything and I'll give him a spanking he won't soon forget."

The keeper was waving now. Mort

didn't wave. Mouse *couldn't* wave. He was still holding his soda pop and he only had the one hand.

"I found you," said the keeper. "I found you, I found you." He was smiling so hard his glasses fell off.

He stepped onto the deck. He had a package under his arm.

"I have something for you," he said. He opened the package very carefully. It was Mouse's missing arm.

Mouse dropped his pop he was so surprised.

"Here, let me put it on," said the keeper.

"Whoa! Wait a minute there, big boy," said Mort. "I'm the one who puts people back together. You come here and flip these veggies."

The keeper did as he was told and

pretty soon Mort had Mouse's right arm just where it ought to be. Mouse wriggled his fingers. Ah, the joy of pins and needles!

"Thank you," said Mouse. "Both of you."

"I was going to send it, but there weren't enough stamps," said the keeper. "I had to wait until pay day to buy some. That's when I got the idea."

"Yikes!" said Mouse. "Did I hear you say you had an idea?"

The keeper nodded proudly. "Yes," he said. "I guess it was all those years of talking to you. Do you want to know what it was?"

"We're all ears," said Mouse.

"I got my pay check and I quit."

Mouse and Mort stared at the keeper.

"You quit?"

"Uh-huh," said the keeper.

"Unbelievable! said Mouse. He roared with laughter. Mort snorted with glee.

"You see," said the keeper. "I learned a lot from you, Mouse. When you were gone, I missed you so much, I found myself talking about you to the other prisoners. I told them the story of your daring escape. Only the *un*dangerous ones, of course. I didn't want to give the dangerous ones any ideas."

It was about then that Mort remembered his manners. "Here, let me do that," he said, taking the spatula from the keeper. "You pull up a chair. Will you stay for lunch?"

"Thank you," said the keeper. His eyes lit up. "Such colorful food!" he said. "Nothing at jail was this colorful."

"You can say that again," said Mouse. And do you know what's for dessert? Chocolate tiramisu."

They all had a good laugh. But the chocolate tiramisu reminded the keeper of something and his face grew thoughtful. That's one of the problems with learning how to think. You become thoughtful.

"What's up?" asked Mouse.

"It's the warden," said the keeper. "The day before I left, I accompanied him on his rounds. He looked into your cell and saw the tin mouse lying there and do you know what he said?

He said, 'I'm glad Ned Mouse has a cold. It serves him right for stealing my dessert.'"

There was nothing to say. The three of them just shook their heads and tried to imagine how anyone could be so mean, so stingy and so very, very spiteful.

"I'm sure glad you're back together," said the keeper. "Pretty clever of me to find you, huh?"

"Amazing," said Mouse. "Considering that all you had to go on was the address."

"I know," said the keeper enthusiastically.

"And speaking of addresses," said Mouse, a concerned look on his face. "You didn't give ours away, I hope."

The keeper got a mischievous

twinkle in his eye. "I'm pretty good at keeping things," he said. "Especially secrets."

The keeper took a job at Morty's Doll Factory. In the shipping department. He was very good at shipping things, too. When Mort first offered him the job, he told him that the employees had voted to work a shorter week so that they could spend more time with their families.

"Oh," said the keeper, hanging his head. "Then I guess I can't work there."

"Why not?"

"Because I don't have a family."

"Oh, what a tree you are," said Ned Mouse with great compassion. "And you are as stout-hearted as an oak. We will be your family, Keep. Mort and I."

And so, the keeper stayed on. Like the big tree that he was, he put down roots.